Here's To Another Year

A collection of poetry
A journal
A bookshelf decoration
A home for doodles

Jesse B. Simmons

Disclaimer: Poetry is neither fiction nor nonfiction and should be taken with a grain of salt.

*I dedicate this collection to those who shaped my life for better or worse
and
anyone who hasn't decided if they like loving themselves yet.*

If you can't bring yourself to write in books, enjoy the extra space, soak in the emptiness that we seem to severely lack in the world today.

If you love writing in books, I dare you to write in the extra space, write your own poems, responses, notes, draw your own illustrations. Make a journal so filled, it's ok when you're hollow.

The Days That won't end

M	T	W	Th	F	Sat	Sun

Daughter of Demeter
You don't die in the Fall
You live in the cinnamon that floats
In homemade apple cider,
You aren't dead in the Winter
You live in the holiday wine glasses
And the trees set up with lights.

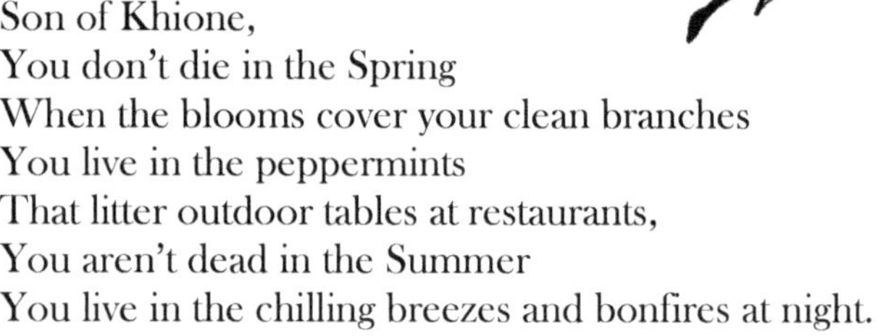

Son of Khione,
You don't die in the Spring
When the blooms cover your clean branches
You live in the peppermints
That litter outdoor tables at restaurants,
You aren't dead in the Summer
You live in the chilling breezes and bonfires at night.

I fade in the Spring,
When everything else breathes in new life
I exhale heavily through sleepless nights
Flowers bloom, and let out a sweet scent—
It smells like blood rushing too quickly
Through my veins
A heart that pumps like the construction outside my window,
I expire in the Summer
The laughter in the air—
It hides the whimpers that I never let go of
That have to squeeze out
Through my skin.
- Seasonal Depression

If I could be anyone in the world right now
I'd be myself,
But with effortlessly wavy, raven-colored hair
Bright, brown eyes that put copper to shame
A purpose in life
A plan
Goals
And maybe my name would be Camille
I would have a fat ass
Hot abs, tits, pecs, booty
Be a huge beast, and skinny and petite,
Just so I could feel like myself.
    -    Shapeshifting

I sit in front of the mirror and put on my face
I can barely catch the nervous flitting of my own pupils
In my reflection
But when I do, I hold them in the palm of my hand
And skip them like rocks
So no one can see the fear, the doubt inside
My painted eyes—
A small canvas covered in art
On a wall of skin that doesn't match the vision
I am so desperate to actualize,
I darken my eyebrows, my lashes, my jawline
I stain my lips
And finally meet my eyes
How many years have I avoided the inner child I see in the
reflection?
I put on a wig and pause—
Beautiful, feminine, masculine,
Is it enough to go outside
To be seen?
Not yet.
So I keep practicing.
-       Drag me out tonight

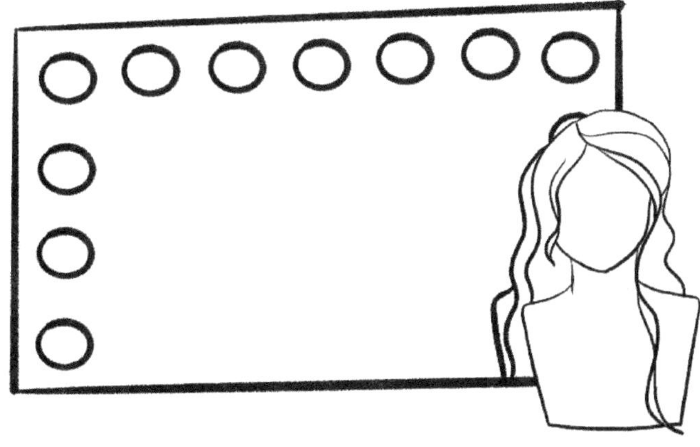

A part of me will always love the occult
It reminds me of high school
When we would sit in the car after movies
And talk about the sex demons we might summon—
A last resort sort of date,
Because even though it was verging on the height
Of the moon
And we jumped
Anytime dark figures walked next to our car,
We weren't ready to go home yet.

Don't stop
Balancing on curbs
Jumping in puddles
Picking up leaves,
Don't let go
Of the child you grew up as
Whom you may think was lost or left,
It's the most original you've
Ever been.
    -    And still are

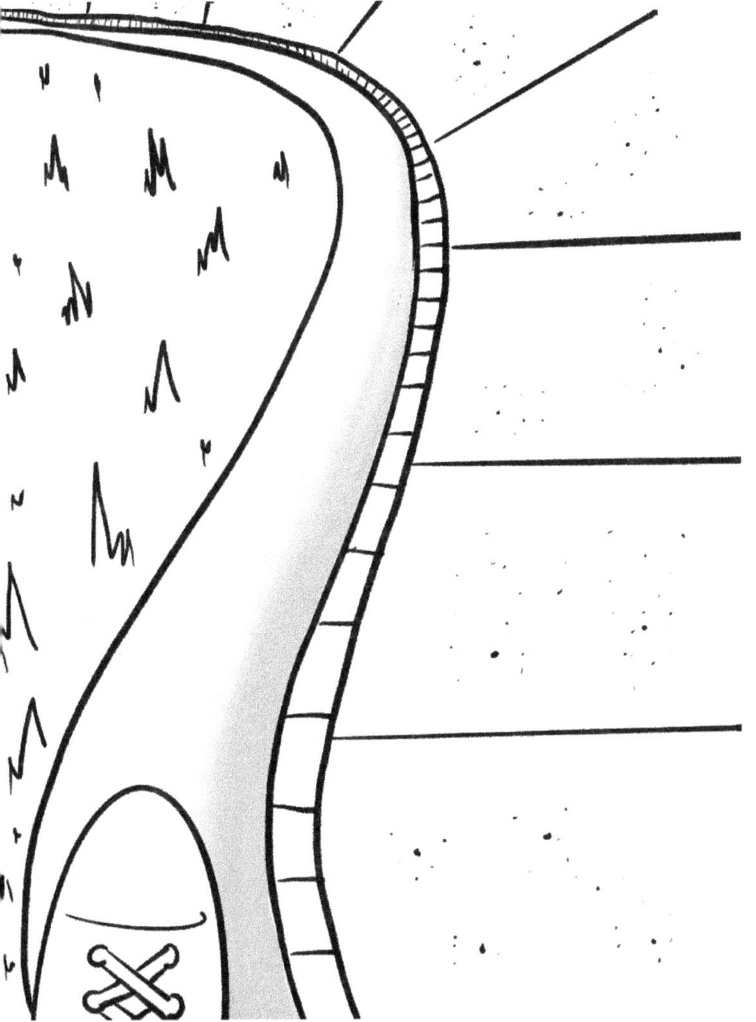

You don't deserve any mistreatment

From anyone—

Not even yourself,

I don't care
If they justify
Blame
Storm off
I don't care if you just had a fight
If you said something hurtful
It doesn't matter if you were the villain today
Which I doubt you were,
You still don't deserve to be
Mistreated.

There's no weak link in a chain,
If any threaten to break
It's the stress—
Not the structure.

Your greatest strengths are your greatest weaknesses, which
makes you the best and worst person on the team, and
they need you.

-    Our flesh is not metal and our bones are not tools

A dentist job would pay the bills
Give me a house with tall ceilings and windows—
A cut above the other cookies
A Christmas tree and lights
That gleam a landmark on suburban roads at night,
But all I want
Is something that'll keep me warm at night
When comforters and heating aren't enough.
  -       A dream, not a blanket

Dreams
Never really die.

When strangers stab at them
They dodge they run they jump they survive,
It's when people you trust
Lull you into a moment that feels safer than it is
Convince you not to want it,
They get bloodied and bruised.

They lie at the base of your body
Barely breathing
Limp and raw.
-      You believed them

Dreams are the dazzling bits of starlight
That fall from the sky so we can carry them
With us every day,
Something that's real
But not tangible enough
For others to touch.

Warm whispers
Like transparent spring water
Rinse the questions out of my mind,
They know better
Than to leave me with my thoughts
For too long.

When you picture rain,
Is it a sprinkle or a downpour?
Is there wind?
Are you standing in it
Or watching from the window?
Perhaps you just listen
From the comfort of your bed.

When you think of snow
Are you walking through falling flakes?
Slipping on ice?
Or hiding from hail?
Will it storm
Inside or outside
Of you?

I'm having a storm,
A violent wind that screams in your ears
A torrential downpour that weighs down the roof
A thunder that shakes the place we call home.

Yes, the storm will pass
The birds will chirp again
The sun will come out,
But the silence I sit in afterwards
In the damp
In the din
In my head
Is where you should be worried.
- No one worries after the storm

I'd like to think I love meeting new people–
Collections of seashells and crystals
Spilling out of my pockets and arms,
But some I'll hold onto like shards of glass
Sticking out of my back
Though I won't pretend
I don't go looking for that sometimes,
And then there are those
I've gotten so tired of fighting with
Who want nothing or less
For anyone else
Than they have or wish themselves
Who are so scared of losing what isn't meant to be kept,
And I can only find solace
In the fact that none of us will exist one day
And it'll almost be like
None of this happened at all.
  -     Out of my hands and off of my shoulders

You say you're a bad person,
But I've never seen you do a bad thing–
Only mistakes.

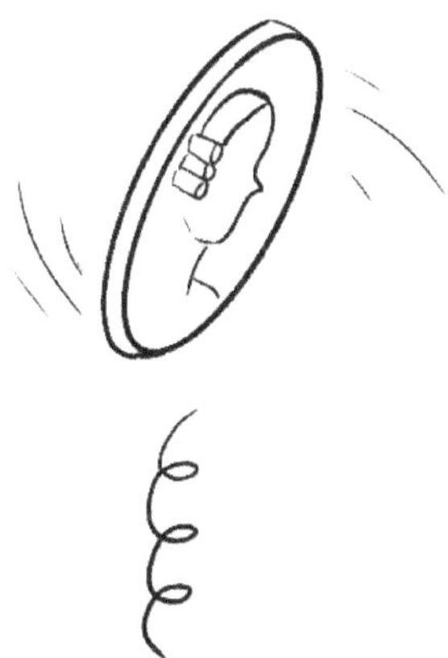

You say you're a good person
But I've only ever seen you hurt people
Mistakes you call them
Then apologies.

Yes, I want change
I want something better
And not just for myself,
But I still grew up here
A push-pin in a map
Identities, cultures, philosophies unexplored,
We all did
It's all we know,
I used to expect myself to innately be better
To know everything about being minoritized
So, I won't shame
For absorbing surroundings,
But I will question
Anyone who chooses not to change
For the better.

Don't open my closet
It isn't skeletons you'll find—
Well,
Maybe just mine.

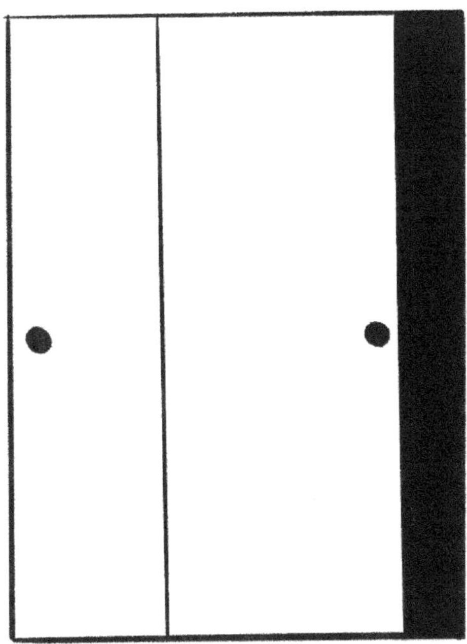

I feel all emotions
Or none at all,
My happy medium
Is escape.

I stopped telling you things
Because I got tired of you telling
Me what I cared about was silly,
Which shouldn't even be considered a bad thing.

You never quite figured out
That it wasn't about you.

Me neither.

I'm done telling jokes
It's time for straight trauma dumping.

Sometimes I want something bad to happen just as much
as something good.
Sometimes
Something is all that matters.

If we keep erasing
Our past,
How much of us
Will be left?
Or is that the point?

What if I'm so anxious because my heart is slow and needs
the extra boost to keep me alive, What if I treat my anxiety
and I die because my heart doesn't pump enough without it,
What if I'm not funny without being mentally ill (which
matters because what do I offer my friends if not
entertainment), What if I'm an entirely different person,
What if that's a bad thing, What if that's a good thing (which
might be worse), What if it doesn't matter what happens,
What if
I'm ok in the end?

What if I give myself permission just to survive.

What if the world is as terrible as I think?

I'll be ok in the end.
    -     or maybe I won't

Unfortunately, it seems you have two cavities.

Oh,
I say.

But all I can hear is a begging in the back of my brain
To burrow into
The newfound holes in my teeth
Warmed by my steady breath
And safe behind a strong jaw.
    -        Retreating into myself

I hide in my room
Not because I want to be alone
But because I want someone
To come get me,
They'll always know where I am.

I want to knock on doors
And invite people out
To talk, to eat, to live,
But the door feels more like a wall
Than an entrance.

I have made the extremely well-informed and calculated decision to drop off the face of the planet.
- Let me go somewhere no one will find me

I live my life
Safely
Quietly
Slowly
Anything
That can prolong
The wick a little bit longer,
I want to know
What happens next.

But I'm a jester
In control,
Not a clown
But a mime
Putting myself in an invisible box
With a lock that I can't see,
I don't act
I don't start
I don't change
Because maybe I don't want to know
What happens next.

But I want to want to,
I really do.

Money is meant to satiate
The rumblings of your stomach
To fill the cavity of your chest
With flowery ornaments
And cover your sensitive skin
With satin,
It's meant to fill your needs,
Still,
I'm hungrier after I get a paycheck
Than when I run out.

How can it be
That as devoid of emotion
I may find myself
I'm never
Empty
Of want.

I have no concept of money or time
They don't have answers for me,
If I wasn't so anxious
I might give all my money away
And then die.
    -     Actually, that's what we all do

The fireflies
My parents caught as kids
Flaunted glowy assets
Decorated jars for minutes of awe
Or were danced around like a dreamy movie sequence
Just enough light to play in the dark,
At night I watch metal pillars illuminate
Buzzing their brightness
As if we could miss them walking by
Just enough light to see someone behind you,
My shadow smudges under
Engineered luminosity—
Streetlights
Guide my way home.
-     They tell me it's a different world now

Would you rewind time
Just to go back through it the same way?

If no,
Then why do we repeat
The same year over and over again?

If yes,
Well
Lucky you.

Where is the pinprick of earth
That tickles the bottom of the sky,
Where is the top of the mountain?

I could lay my body halfway up—
A fossil, half sunken in mud
To serve as a warning to others
And proof that I tried,
Or I can trust my brain, forget my body—
I know the summit is up there.
-     If I saw the sunrise would I be impressed?

It wasn't until
My legs grew long,
And my eyes grew heavy
That I thought to take a break,
Breathe.

I'm not one to think I can't turn around
Or take a path less trodden,
But every direction looks the same,
Never-ending
Immense
And miserable.

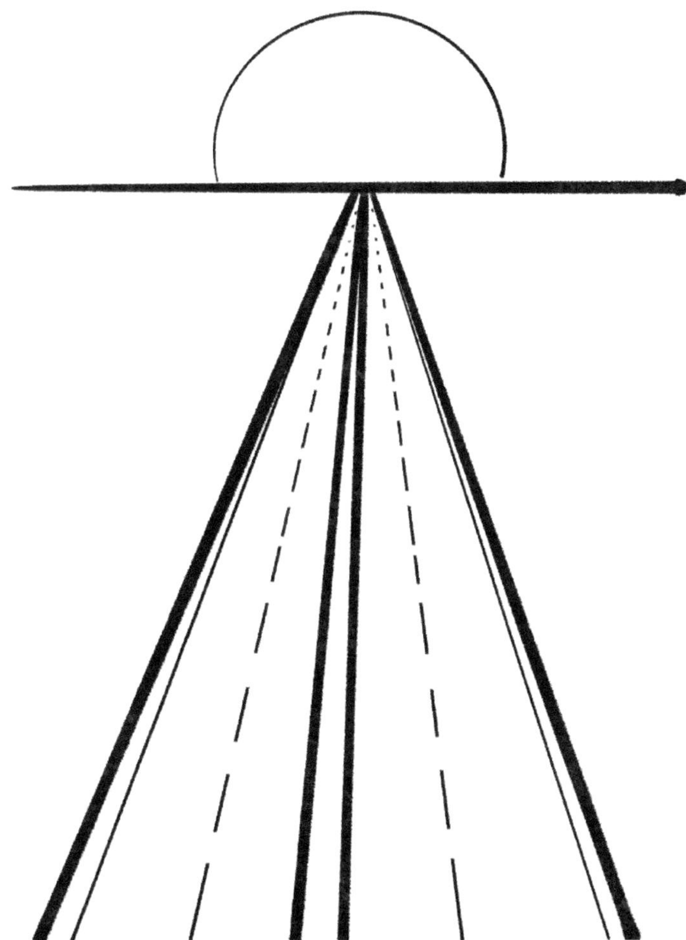

I love you
Mom and Dad,
It was from you who I learned about my culture
It was you who passed down anxiety
It was you who picked me up when I was down
It was you who taught me to suppress my intuition
It was you taught me to love
It was you who taught me how
I could never see the world,
I love you
Mom and Dad,
But sometimes I hate the way you love me.

They love
By giving,
But I love
By not taking,
Even if the love pours
From a fire hose
We both go to bed
With nothing.

My bedroom is always cluttered
A depression room made by hand, locally sourced
To show off to my friends,
But to me it's a room of gifts
A collection of habits
From every little mistake you blew up on me for,
As long as there's a path to my bed and the door
It's all good.
- Things you didn't mean to give,
and I didn't mean to take

I land in the hands that hurt me
Because I recognize them
And because I know
They've been through the same thing.

I'm good,
I am good
I am
I promise,
It just takes me
Longer to get out of bed
More pints of ice cream,
It just takes more
To keep me going now.

Life is like taking a breath
Or many,
Easy subconsciously
But hard overthought,
I'm aware my worry doesn't keep the clock ticking
Though it doesn't stop me from trying
To pump my lungs like bicycle tires
In the middle of the night,
I've been told to take it a day at a time
But I need something smaller
Something I almost won't ever notice.
- A breath at a time

The Days That

i stopped holding my breath

M	T	W	Th	F	Sat	Sun

After
Twenty years of drowning,
I discovered
There is no up from down
No direction
Will lead me to break the surface.

But lost isn't so bad
Because I realized
I was breathing
Underwater
The whole time.

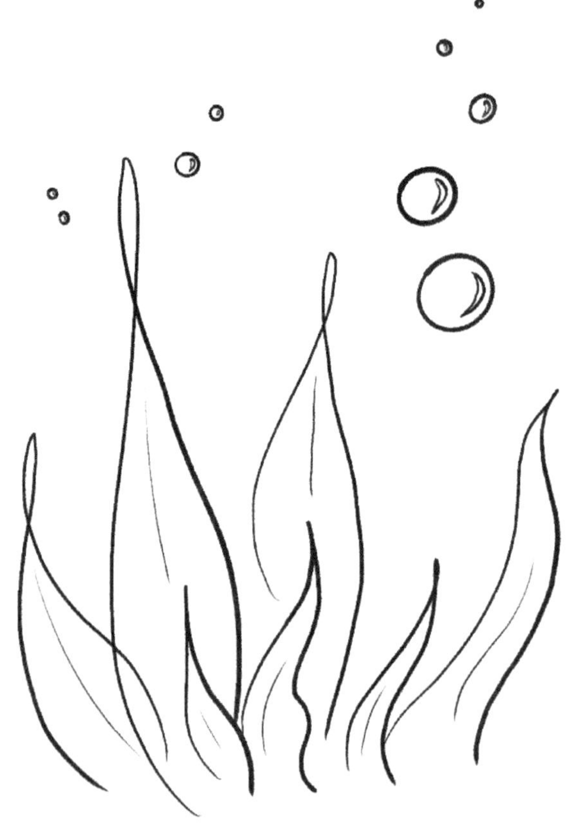

Y'all.
If you have depression and anxiety
And something small makes you
Want to lose your shit
Take a sick day–
Be sick
Drink some tea and take a nap,
You sick sexy bastard.
- A love letter

Here's to another year
Of sinking into concrete sidewalks
Holding your breath when people pass by
Singing until you see someone staring
Drinking enough to love the eyes that watch you dance
Eating until you don't fit into your jeans
Sitting like a chameleon
In the background
Watching and listening—
Hoping no one sees you staring,
Then shedding
And living anyways.

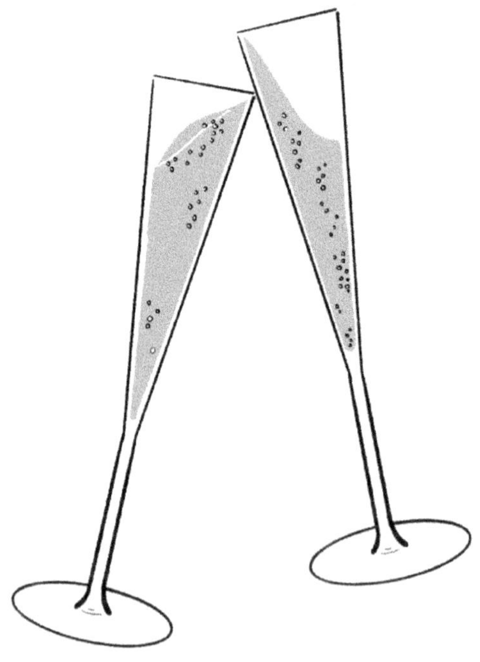

When reading a book
Don't forget to breathe
The words in,
Let them soak
Before you gobble them down
And misplace the parts
That made you starve
For them in the first place.

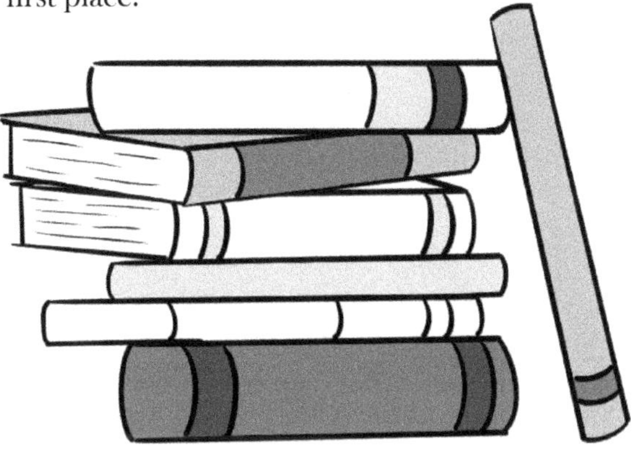

I'm not a camper,
I don't live in a cabin
Or walk through the woods
Where I can't get a signal,
I'm not drawn to the absence
Of warmth and comfort from my bed,
But that doesn't stop me
From dousing my clothes
With campfire smoke
Or roasting marshmallows
On my deck with the sliding door cracked open,
I still look up at the stars at night
Even if I can only see a few of them.

The outdoors is everywhere,
I want to fill my lungs
With being able to breathe again,
Even when I can't get away.

Everyone is a gambler.

Falling is the flip of a coin
Churning the air as you plummet,
Whichever side you land on
Seals your fate.

Fate is when you want the answer you landed on,
Adventure is when you turn it over.

A game of chance
Is letting go of the need to win
Every battle,
Fate gives us the win
When we need
It most.

Realization hits me
Like a long walk in a dense fog
That leaves dewdrops like love nips
Up and down my arms—
They tell me secrets when I listen
When I have the energy to care,
The cold drops drip so confidently off the top of my nose
As if I should've known all along
That I need to pick experiences like berries off a bush
Not plants I want to have already grown.

And in the mist
I've lost sight
Of the
Skyscrapers, schools, McMansions, price tags, suits, ties,
pearls, dinner parties, paychecks, strangers
That insist on telling me otherwise.
- How many times can I pretend to be surprised by this

He grows jasmine
In the darkest
Hedge labyrinths
So I can guide myself
Back home
By smell.

The earthy spice
I breathe in
From my ginger scallion
Love letter to myself
Reminds me
To share what I love,
To look for connection
Instead of competition.
-       Sharing a meal

You wear flowers
That bring out the color of your eyes—
But when I go in for a deeper look I see
Mirrors that only serve to reflect back my own questions
When all I want is to know what you think of me right here
and now
And before my heart can beat any harder
I steer my vision back to your flowers
The ones that I swear must be a mask;
Petals shiny and soft
Stamens protruding perkily—
They can't be real
But your skin radiates floral aromas,
Maybe it's just you.
-       There's just something about him that feels so natural

Are you getting my lovesick letters?
The ones with smudged ink
And not-so-witty one liners,
I'd put your address on them
If I knew what it was.

Why the letters?
Well I'll do anything desperate and dramatic
That won't actually help
Me get any closer to meeting someone
I'll do anything to prove to myself that you don't exist.
-       Love of my pathetic life

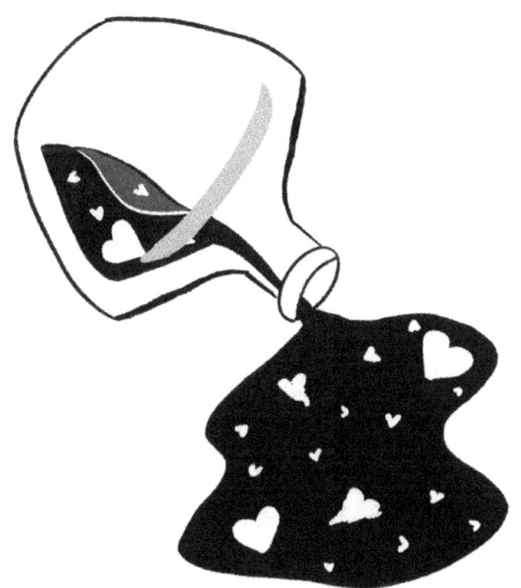

The hot air
He breathes out
Into the cold
Around us
Makes a steam cloud
That draws my eyes
To his lips
Every. Damn. Time.
  - Tell me your life story, I'm listening, promise

Your angry words drip like red hot cinnamon syrup
From your mouth,
I know I should be angry too
Or maybe I should apologize,
But I just want to feel the
Crackling spice roll down my throat
So I can feel your colors
In my chest.
- 	I pick fights for the fun of it, for the sexiness

Why am I alive?

Why are any of us alive?

I wasn't asking
For a sense of purpose—
I'm saying
It's unfair.

You're glad you're still here, right?
- 　　Floating

What if I fall in love?
Don't.

What if I fall in love?
Do you want to?

What if I fall in love?
You won't even know it's happening—
It doesn't feel like falling
It feels like being caught.

My crossed arms aren't asking to be pulled apart,
I'm not looking at your lips
I'm watching your teeth.

I don't need a hero or a villain
We aren't characters
With roles to play—main or side
Why can't we both walk through the woods
Dodge the big bad wolf
And pick flowers?
-       And then like kiss and stuff

Anger is a way to communicate pain
Sadness is a way to feel it,
But the source of the sensation
Has always been you.

I don't think I'll ever understand you
I don't think I want to.

How do you not know you're hurting me?
I think maybe you do.

Conclusions jump
Like fire from my mouth
In the moth-sized pause between sentences,
I know I should
Let the silence hang there
For a short icy second
Let my ears sculpt the sounds into meaning,
But I want a conversation
Like gunshots of a machine gun.
-     learning to listen

Words fly off our lips like birds taking flight

Then land like boulders
And weigh down the air
Like the asphyxiation after a confession,
A question tickles my tastebuds
Like static behind my eyes—
Was it worth it?
- I regret that what I needed to say hurt you, but not
  that I said it

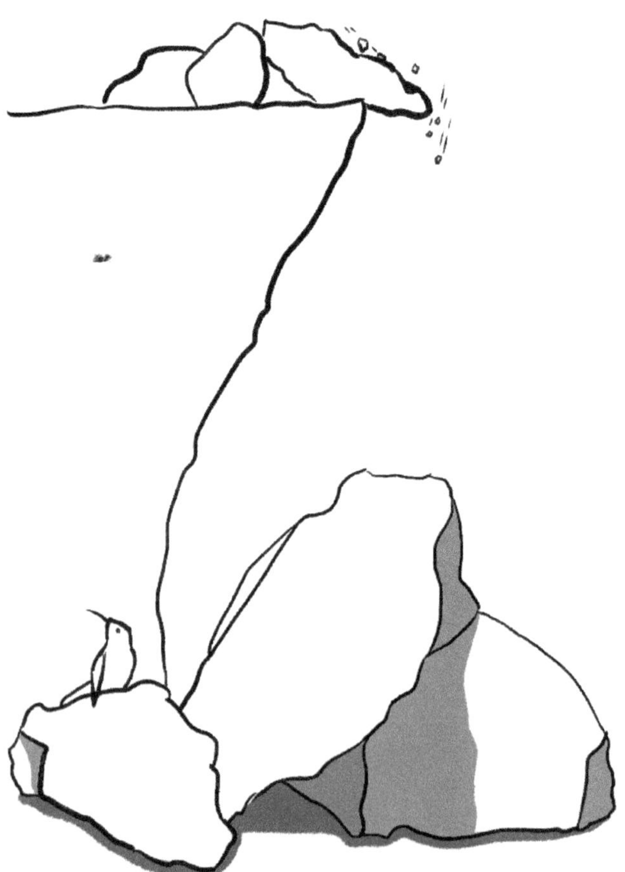

I envy peacocks—
Not for their feathers
Or stature,
They're pompous and violent
Their mating is too scary
To call love,
But they don't hide or pretend—
At least they're honest
In their actions.

I expect people to get mad at me
They should
I think,
I suppose I might be the villain
In their story
Just as I am in mine.

Hey, how are you today?
Oh ya know
I made a mistake.

So now I'm upset
That I'm alive.

I rend my flesh into shapes like a flower
So even in passing I could please someone,
Sure, maybe I'm the problem—
Always wanting to be the breeze
To cool off a humid day
But it's just as hard to bend my body
Backwards into a bridge for you to step on
As it is for me to stand up for myself,
Go home,
And replace guilt
With sleep.

I may never understand
The dogfights to prove your worth
To gain respect where it wasn't freely given,
Why would you want to be in the minds of people
Who never saw you as a person
In the first place?

Sometimes as I walk through my days
It isn't until I find myself
At the top of a tower or hill over a city
That I find air fresh
Enough to remember
I'm afraid of heights
And the world is real around me
Not just a film my eyes project to my brain.
    -    What does it take to remember I'm still alive?

I wonder if I'll die when I'm done living
Or when life is done with me,
I don't know which is longer
Or harder.

I wish I knew
When I started believing
That when something was too hard to say
Out loud
It never happened.

I wish a diary
Was secret enough
To hold monstrosities.

-       Some secrets aren't meant to stay that way

It's okay to be scared
There's a lot to be scared of,
Being scared keeps you alive,
But it shouldn't keep you from
Living.

Emotions are part of the experience
Like lemon with water
Or sweat at a rave,
Emotions are part of your memories,
Even if your trip ended in tears
Even if it wasn't what you wanted or expected,
It was everything it needed to be.

At the same time,
Why romanticize your life?
It doesn't need to be perfect
Not every moment will teach you,
But don't beat yourself up
For having feelings,
I want you to love them
As I've learned to miss them
When they hide from me.

It's ok
If you want more from life
Than you were allotted
Than you thought before,
It isn't selfish to want things for yourself.
- I want to be happy and safe, now more than ever
  before

Here's to all the artists
Who haven't found their style
The writers who start a new project every two months
The poets with small vocabularies
The musicians still learning music theory,
Here's to all the creators of the world
Who have to fight everyday
To practice their craft
Who may never catch up
To the idols, influencers, fame, or fortune,
Here's to the people who can't find themselves yet.

I cover pages with shitty poetry
Because I have a shitty vocabulary
And a lot of shit to say.
   -     And I want to say shit a lot

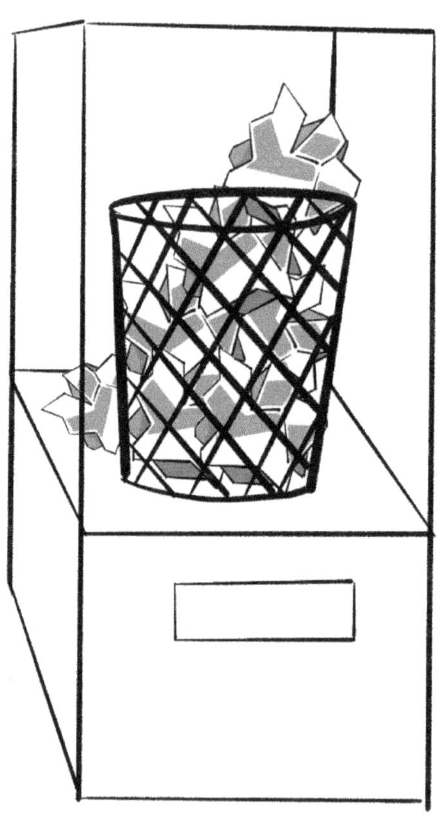

Don't let word count or size
Dictate the value of a piece
Art doesn't need to weave starlight before our eyes
I've written pages of love letters to no one
And small stamps of three, four, five words
That save my life over and over.
- 　　Just make what you want

Bumbling blathers
Escape from my fumbling
Quivering lips
Words over-chewed
And under enunciated,
I tell my stories
Afraid of being heard
But more afraid of not speaking.

I can't keep walking by people who need help
What are you going to do about it?
I'll write.
-        Will it be enough?

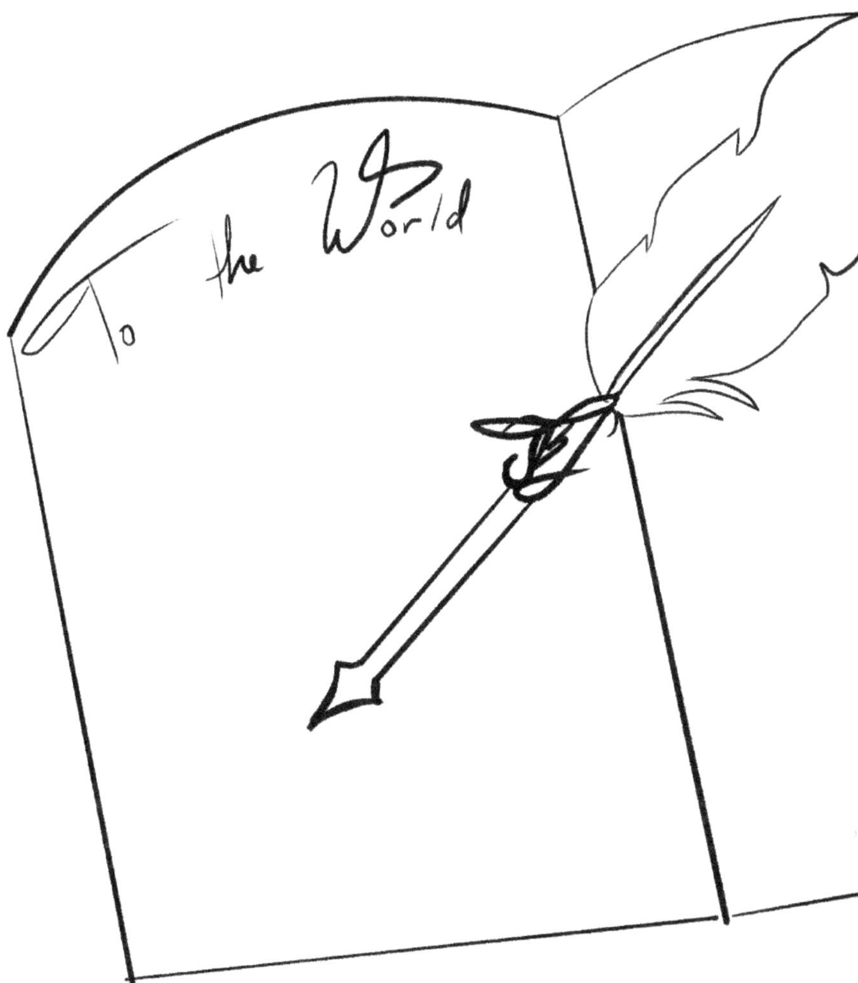

If I make something
That people can love,
It won't matter
If they don't love me.

-       Except it does matter

Growing up, I wanted to be a pop idol,
A sheep herder,
A bottle designer
For a winery in Italy.

Somehow I haven't ended up in any of these places—
Not yet anyway.

I guess I'm a poet now
Whatever that means.

But I find myself looking for quicksaves, replays—
To make good and bad decisions
Say the right and wrong things.

There could be a multiverse
Where I'm living an infinite number of lives
But who cares if another me is doing some crazy shit
If I never get to see what it's like?

I want a library with trinkets and stained glass windows
Where every book holds a piece of my soul
And to spend an eternity reading each one.

How many lives can I fit in mine?
-      Earnestly

The Days That don't fit in my chest

M	T	W	Th	F	Sat	Sun

Maybe if I kept my mouth shut
Nothing would've changed.

What's stopping you?
I don't know,
I want it
A little bit

A lot sometimes,
But I don't want to build
A future

More than
I want
To hide
Here and now.
-    Back where
I started

I want that fireworks moment
Where I reach up on my tippy toes
Just close enough to
Touch the colors and flame
And still not get burnt,
Nor would I care if I did.
-      Playing with fire

Sometimes your fireworks
Are rustling leaves
Snoozed alarms
Mere afterthoughts
For the people you want to care the most,
But are they big enough for you?

I watch a sparkler fizzle at my feet—
It looks like my heart
Not allowed to love
Too loudly
Too proudly.

A tiny firework in the tall grass
Won't start a fire, it won't start much of anything.

It's a muted spark
Talked over by friends and forest critters
Overlooked by turned backs and held hands.

When the star shower fell from your hand
I couldn't decide if I should pick
It back up--nurse the fire or
Hide the unruly honesty
Behind my lonely thighs.
- Will you snuff this one out
Or should I

My first love
Was a shovel,
My first rebound
A rubber band
That shot me deep
Into the earth
A dark cavern I could sleep and hide in—
A second blow to the heart
I wasn't sure I would survive.

And now?

I'm not sure I did,
I haven't been able to let anyone in
The way I did that year.
-      Not even myself

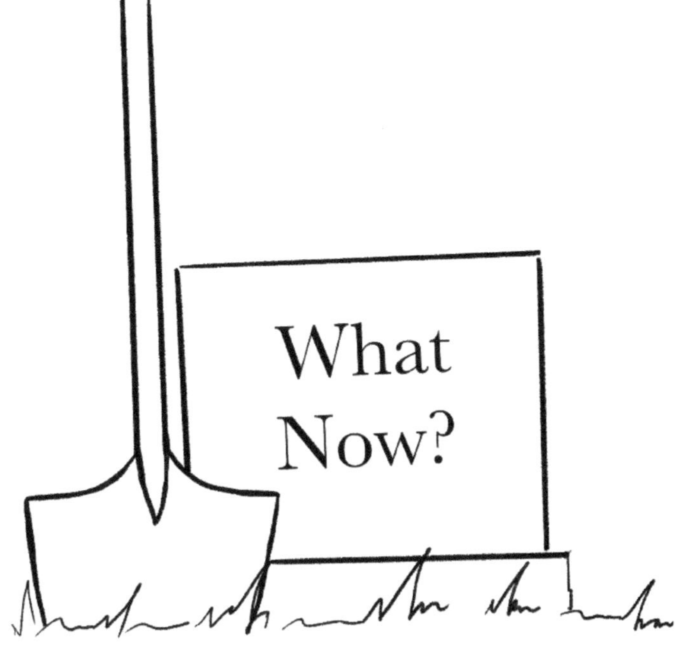

Time stopped.

I know it did
Because my heart
Didn't beat a single time before it was over—
I remember sweaty palms and shaky hands
--Mostly the feelings--
Regret, anxiety, guilt
As if somehow I would no longer be
Allowed to grow up the way I had been
As if by rejecting expectation
I would transform into
A victim
A lonely soul
A pile of dust to be swept under the rug.

We didn't talk about it
--I don't acknowledge any words we did say—
Though it was still big in all the little ways
Like looking for the new silverware drawer
in your childhood home
Like donating clothes from high school
Like realizing you don't have a best friend anymore
Things you can know and expect and nearly prepare for
But feeling it?
Is fatal.
-     Coming out

Men are not something we have in common
I'm not here to be your boy friend with a boyfriend.

We are a blanket of flame,
Candles linked by shared wax
That keep alight
Even when many are washed away,
The dark is a never-ending fight
That melts the wax over lifetimes,
But the drips that drop to the bottom of the heap
Build the next ones higher
Just a little closer to liberation—
Not a collection of mounds
But an interconnected range.
    -    Generations

The "dark" is the patriarchy by the way.

I wish
I could inherit your love of life,
There are stars that sit behind your eyes
Like you're made of the cosmos
And the sunset is still the most beautiful thing
You've ever seen
Every night.

I wish
I could find joy in losing
Like you when people you love get to win,
It's as if your happiness comes in the shape of a bubble
And is filled by everyone inside of it.

I'm worried that when you're gone
That piece won't live on in me
And I might never see it again.
-      So I'll save it here forever

She loves life enough for the both of us
And maybe
At least for now,
It's enough.

Politeness and respect
Shouldn't be confused
With conformity and servitude,
Don't pretend you know what other people want.

Stereotypes
Make us hard workers, intellectual
Eloquent, graceful even
To fill in minority profiles in STEM industries,
We are pocket pets
Whittled to fit cleanly into white pockets
But what happens when we underachieve?
What happens when we want lives
Outside of quiet professionalism?
What happens when we're like everyone else?
-	Model minority

I am made of paper,
A statue held together by flour, water,
And pages of books where men kiss.

On the bad days I'm left outside in the rain
Soaked so that the smallest things might rip me apart,
On the good days I'm covered in bark—armor
I'm safe
But no one can see me,
On the best days
Which is to the say the ones I love for better or worse—
I'm on display
With tales—a history
Inked into my skin like tattoos
So that someone might see me and think
                              Wow
I want to live like that one day.

Gender
Is a tightrope
A spiderweb beneath my feet,
I've landed somewhere I don't know if I belong,
But we're so high up
I'm afraid to move around
I want a new perspective
But I don't want to fall.

The sun on my face is more heavy than warm
So at night I go outside and goosebumps rise up my arms,
I wonder if Artemis is looking down on me
I wonder if she even would,
In the day, sweat pervades my shoes
Swelling the spongy material
That protects me over blistering concrete
Then at night I leave them inside,
I'm meant to cherish my time in the sunlight
As an artist
As a son of Apollo
But if Apollonian music is a child of the day,
Then why do we hear it all night?
Garage bands practicing their sets for the weekend
Vibrations from car speakers
As they zip down neighborhood streets
Why does inspiration strike in bed
Before the sun rises again?
Why does whimsy strike past twelve?
Why do I like the light of the moon so much more?

Because I was born with this body
I am a son of the day who lives in the night,
And I couldn't
Or shouldn't dare
Hope to be a daughter of the moon.

I'm not afraid of my own masculinity,
...who told you that?

The scorching rage
The red-hot coals
Hate:
A thin membrane
Around my body
To try and keep
The cool empty longing
The solitary vigil
The ice-cold fear
Sitting inside
Warm.

We associate fire with anger, rage, and passion
But mine flows like water--
It's a slow swell
Like the filling of a pond,
It warms up gradually
Into a rolling boil
And just as quickly
Drains away
Still wild and bubbling,
But leaves only sediments
In its wake.

We let anger hang between us.

Let it swing like a pendulum.

We stand on either side of the oscillations
And step closer
Daring the wrecking ball to graze our soft stomachs,
We ask it to knock us over
A martyr's vindication,
Then we get back up
And call it love.

They have a smothering love
A love that doesn't listen
A love that doesn't care
It isn't soft or tender
It isn't fair or safe
It isn't what I thought it would be
But it's enough to love them back.
-        A love that wouldn't even entertain my self-
          destruction

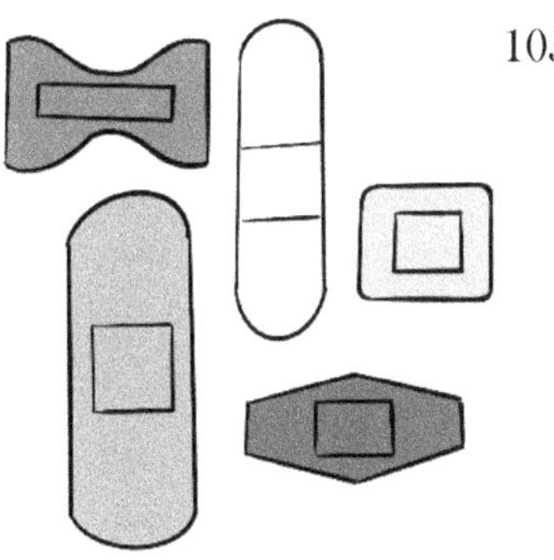

My parents read me stories,
Some already written
Others made up—
I was glued to books
Sported colorful Band-Aids
On each finger, like rings.

I wanted to know our stories
Asked my grandma, her eldest kids
When I was brave enough
But never got more than a few lines at a time—
Maybe I'm wrong
But it felt like it tired them
Like they were reaching for something on a high shelf
Without looking—without knowing if something was really
there.

I don't ask as much now—never more like—
I'm scared,
How do you ask where you came from
When it brings up trauma and loss?
Does wanting to know even make it my business?

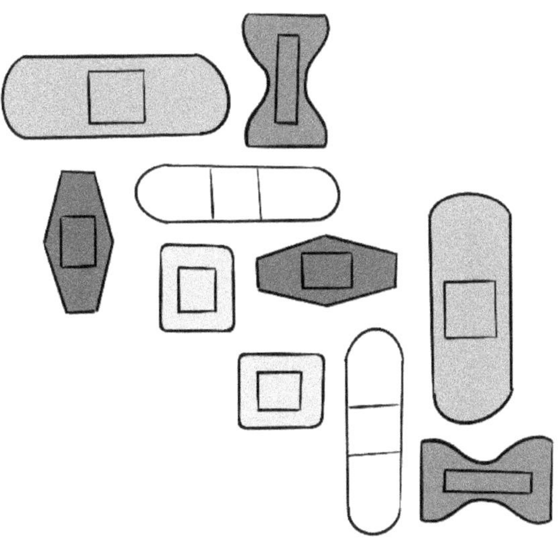

Who takes care
Of you when you've grown up?
I look for more parents
Everywhere I go,
People who know
How to help me
Now.

I dream of meeting you
Of knowing you want me,
But the hot
The sweat
The breath
The flesh and blood,
Knowing what you want from my body,
That comes in my nightmares.
-        How much am I willing to sacrifice for a man?

I'm not the most grateful person
I get caught up in the worst of the world
But after a late night of crying a puddle into my pillow
I can breathe out a wakened repose
A little bit of relief that lives
In the airy spaces between words,
Like a conversation with the world
No one is listening to,
It's the kind of love
That I wish danced along more words in the English language
The kind that only you can bring out of my body
That makes me love everything around me.
-     Agape

Love might be everything you think it is:
Romance, late nights talking, reaching your goals, spending
time with your family, a swing, a job, a diving board, a fence,

But it's also everything you don't see and won't notice
Because it's everyone all around you,
Everything that's kept you around this long.
- You don't need to understand love to have it;
to enjoy it

The sky's vastness
Its blue without edges
Day or night
Is dizzying freedom,
It's falling
And stillness at the same time.

Some days—
The ones when my mind is furthest from my body—
The ground doesn't feel solid
And gravity threatens to let go of my feet,
The hair on my arms is pulled skyward
As I'm stuck on a rollercoaster without a seatbelt
Falling upwards
Into a cold space
Without a hug or tickle of grass or prickle of concrete.

So I walk, staring at the ground
Which might have been enough
If not for the sea
Because the ocean
Is merely a reflection of the sky,
Even more
Unknown.

I hold people
To anchor myself—
Though they don't often hold me back—
They don't know I need that,
On the warm nights they'll:
Whisper kind words that almost
Convince me the world isn't that scary-
Make jokes like we aren't about to fall off the Earth-
Touch the small of my back
Like I'm not about to go anywhere-

Breathe the air that isn't below my feet-
Give me a spine to lean into
That hasn't yet turned to foam,
They talk about the stars
As if they aren't something to be afraid of
And sometimes
I'll believe them.

-Kenophobia

People pass through here
Like there's somewhere else to go
Like there's a way out,
But I've checked the doors—
Always locked,
So, I sit in front of the tv for another day
And watch fiery silhouettes and kisses in the rain,
I am the wet, dirty street
That reflects the fluorescent lights
That douses the fires
That carries the trashed aftermath,
I am the stage
That watches the chaos, love, and dance
From opening night to final call,
But never the play.

Boys and their drugs—
Their fiery messy hair
Their sandy freckles
Their dark eyes that might eat me alive
Their lips that lay both angels and demons to waste
Their hands that can hold and harm,
Let me feel them all.

I know better, I do,
At least when I want to
I do.

I guide an army
Of silent reapers
Awaiting a war that may never happen,
My soldiers
Born from the pollutants
In my head
Fueled by haunting memories,
Every dark moment
Adds to my barracks.

And I wait,
Grow and wait.

He wasn't expecting an onslaught,
But it's all I knew to give.

The anxiety and tension
That holds my muscles and limbs
Together like sinew,
Is always at odds with the stress
That threatens to tear me apart.

My ribcage
Is held together with strings,
A temporary fix
For the hairline fractures
I collected
By swallowing
Fights
Whole.

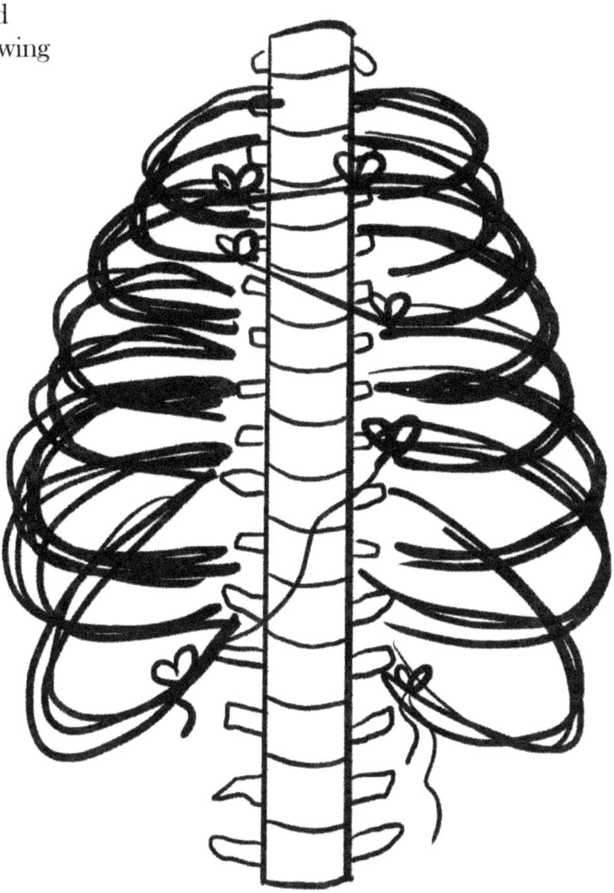

The pressure
In my chest
From the emotions
I keep bottled up
Is an amplifier
So, I can feel my heartbeat
Through my entire body.
-        Do your muscles vibrate under your skin?

I don't need you to tell me how you feel
I already decided how you feel—
You hate me.

I don't start
Every friendship like a bitter hag
I don't only find humor in teasing
Or connection in complaints,
But after years of
Shallow friendships, the resentment builds up,
And it all flows out of my mouth
Like butter.

I cut my chest open
And bleed all over myself
To keep warm.
-      Seeking comfort

When I close my eyes,
It's almost like
I'm the only one
Left in the world,
And I can pursue success
As if it doesn't come at the expense of others.
-      Borrowed responsibility

Sometimes, I take my glasses off
So I can unfocus on the world
So I don't have to see the
Trash on the road
Or the shadows that nip at my footsteps,
I don't want to see lights on
In skyscraper apartments at night
Where happy friends and couples live
When I feel most alone,
I'd rather watch astigmatic blurs of light
As we race down the highway,
I might hide them under the bed or
Hook them around my legs in the dark
So I can't go back into the overwhelm
Until I'm empty enough to find them.

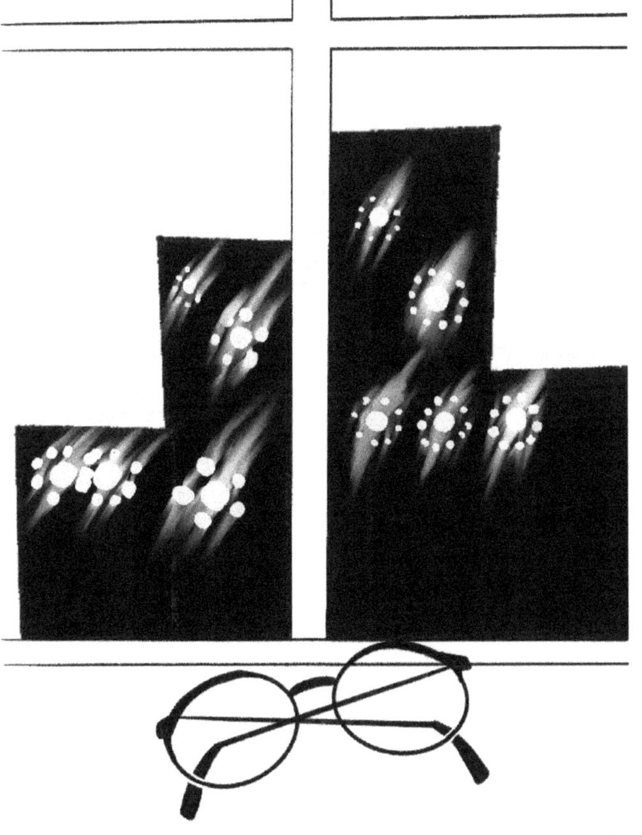

I've spent years
Breaking my dreams
Into tiny creatures
So they can only scare
Me enough
To keep going.

How many hours do we spend
Scraping words from our organs,
Serving our live beating hearts on plates
To cover them with pastel seasonings
And lucid sauces?
At the end of the night
There isn't even a tip on the table—
I'd rather serve my story raw—
Hugged tightly
And still in my chest.

I'm afraid.

That I will only ever know a fraction
Of what my problems are
That the shadows will only get deeper
That I will never understand what in my life made me
Miserable.

I think there's a part of me
That still thinks I need to be fixed.

My roommate jumps ahead in books
To see what happens
She can't wait, or won't,
My dad skips words
To zip through faster
Like a race car burning rubber on the road,
I must take after him if
I rush through my life
Like chapters in a book
Because my jaw won't unclench until I know how it ends.

I was born under two fish
Mother and son circling each other
In a koi pond
Deities of love that can't break their cycle
Around the other,
Even as the borders drop away
To an ocean of stars
They don't need a pond
When they can swim in the sky,
But I've been let loose to the riptides,
I breathe
And wonder if I am meant to be torn apart,
I am at the end of the cycle
And ripples of calm and panic won't change
That I may end in the constellations above me
Or by the curled horns of a ram.
-       Reincarnation

The
Daze

M	T	W	Th	F	Sat	Sun

It's not that I won't be able to get back up, I'm worried I won't want to.

If you see me
With my shoulders hunched
And fists clenched,
If I jump at slight movements
Or flinch at the wind,
Don't worry,
I'm not any more stressed
Than I usually am.

I've filled my bathtub with rum
Because the pine tree outside my window is dying,
I sit in the sugar with stone shoulders,
It feels weird inside the house now
While the world outside falls apart,
So I gather the fallen needles
And pour them over the syrupy ceramic edge,
A golden glaze covers my legs
With brilliant, herbed emeralds,
And I think maybe this sap
Can keep me still
And hold me together.
   -     Don't ask me to go outside today

At least if I'm falling
I'm still going somewhere.

        I don't know where I'm going yet,
        Just that I'm in a rush.

                I've been stuck still
                For too much of my life,
                I just want movement,
                I don't care where
                Anymore.

-     Let me crash if it means something
       will change

Drink the coffee grounds at the end of your cup:
If those images are omens,
Consuming them might give you power
Over your own life.

I stick my head underwater
And try to breathe,
Maybe it'll work this time.
      -      Still not a fish

I'm holding my breath
On my pleather couch
And stare at the wall,
Every couple hours it's like I wake up again
Instead of sleep I collect wasted time.

I hold my breath as I walk past men
Especially if I'm attracted to them,
I don't trust myself
To be able to pretend the world doesn't exist
If I find something I want more than anything.

I think you may be an incubus
From the way you make my body feel,
But I'm not interested in giving you my soul,
I want to chain you to it and fill you with it
I want to be vindicated or loved.

It doesn't take long
To learn which monsters lurk around corners
When you live in the middle of an infested maze,
Cerberus lies West
Gorgons North
Ghosts just a few meters away from my favorite Magnolia,
Our base sits in a cornucopia
Of vanilla bean, jasmine, oranges, and spice,
We venture down our cartographic paths—
So we can keep safe.

The cornucopia is home
Home is familiar,
But we're isolated
And without looking for an exit
We'll never be free from the sights of danger.

The jaws of a cold steel snake
Threaten to crush my body
Until pulp rolls out of micro lacerations
In my summer-tanned skin
The closest I can reach to my Wintered mother,
A humid stormdrop lands on my nose, my eyes
More features they can't place,
I live in this garden
I was born among the flowers here—
But the creatures don't recognize me,
When they're so quick to point out their differences
They're alike in tearing me apart.
    -    Half

They don't let me all the way in
Because I don't look all the way like them
But I don't look like anyone
Except myself,
I am a bowl of blueberries
Mashed to purple-red pulp
We know the blue and green disappear
But that moment lacking recognition,
That's where lines are drawn.

When did things get so out of hand
That you had to tell me
That I deserve my identity?

My identity lives in the culture
I exist in,
Not in the way you think I look or should act.

It's easy to say
It's about having a good life,
Not making money,
Not fame,
Nor success,

    But it seems like
    Without all of those things,
    How many of us are allowed to live a life?

        I know it's about how I live
        Not what I have
        Or what I accomplished,
        But if I start focusing on me
        I'll have to admit to myself
        That I'm not doing ok.

How do you plan a life
When you aren't sure if you get one?
The future I've been given, designed—
How long will it last?
Will it protect me?
What if the person who wrote it
Doesn't look like me
Doesn't love like me
Doesn't know.

They tell you to stand up
Fight for yourself and others
And maybe I should,
But what do I use to fight
When my claws were filed down
So I could eat out of the palm
Of those who fill my food bowl with dust and nails?
- How do you fight when you're already just trying to
survive?

It wasn't supposed to be like this.

I wasn't supposed to lose confidence
When I grew up
The things that used to feel
So clear to me
Are unset cement—
Quicksand under my shoes,
I'm a mime
Pushing at the invisible wall
Standing between myself
And where I want to go
Am I hindered
Or do I just want to be?

I don't know what you're going to say
But I know it'll taste like honey and black pepper–
I can smell it on your breath.

You're trying to help
I know,
But your words haunt me at night
Fireflies and drool dripping from the ceiling
Your voice in my head
Telling me what words to say
Words to believe,
And you sleep soundly
A helper
A hero.
-    Self-Perception

I don't save my ideas
In jars like wishes or blackberry jam.
I don't hide them away
Until my cupboard is overspilling with preserves
They're already magnificent
Without the extra sugar
Why keep that to yourself?
-      Aged like fine lemonade

You can't skip chapters
Or speed through crisp
Yellowed pages in a book,
Just like how flipping through your calendar
Doesn't make the days go by any faster,
You have to sit there
For every bitter moment
Every boring one
Every scary, glorious, addicting scene,
You might not get
A cozy fireplace
Or a mug of tea,
But that's how you live a story yourself.

Is that true?
It is when I say it in my head,
When I feel memories like tiny explosions
Prickling my skin like plastic-crystal freckles.
So yes,
But when you challenge,
When your feelings are hurt,
When it changes your thoughts about me
About our relationship,
Then no,
I just thought the words were pretty.
-       Out like a candle

150

Someone lives in my body
Someone who wants attention
Someone who talks and doesn't listen,
Is it me?

> I love others with jabs and hurt
> In hope that when they hurt me
> It means they might love me too.

-     A mockery of myself

I'm not mad
        When you choose me
        As your emotional dumpster,
        I know it's the only way
        You know how to keep going—
Just tired.
    -    I think I do it too

As a culture
We claim anger is bad—
Conditioned, trained to it
As is sadness
Or envy,
We'll shove them to the bottom of the trash
And toss it in the dumpster
But we don't see the rips in the bag
Or feel it when pieces fall out on our feet
Because that would be embarrassing--tactless.

We can't ignore our bodies are cauldrons
They catch what you drop
And the concoction festers
Like pestilence inside our bodies
And when it comes out, it's a creature of toxic waste
A cartoon enemy.

That's not anger, sadness, or envy
It's a monster of human-creation.
    -    Where does hurt come from?

It doesn't cost
Money
Or years
Of your life
To have compassion.
-    Excerpt of a rant

Do I make myself
More or less bullyable
By bullying myself?

I don't want to let it roll off my back,
I'm not a fucking slide.

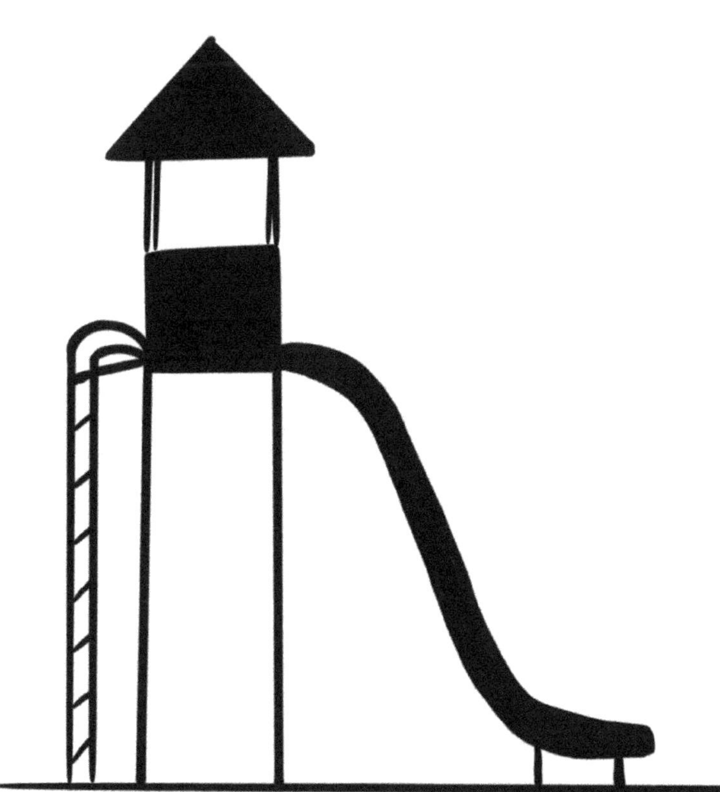

We make the jocks the bullies
Because being hot
Was made to be
A redeemable quality.

We make the jocks the bullies
Because we seem to want to give
The peak of "masculinity"
A free pass.

Our lives are built
On valuing the wasp ridden husk
We call boyhood,
Manhood.
- Bullies are not hot

Creation and
Destruction
Are not enemies,
But twins.

People are
The pinnacle of both,
We are full of hypocrisy
We change our minds
We mean well
We give bad advice
We're emotional
We're confused
We're prideful because we're ashamed
We're not heard so we don't listen
And we live our whole lives
In the human condition.
- You can simplify people if you want, but I probably won't

My lungs are brimming
With liquid steel
Diffused in light-polluted smoky cityscapes
My stomach is lined
With brambles that crack sidewalks
Where trees once stood
Nurtured by the early onset of chaos weather,
I can't finish digesting
The panic
When the days flip between
A man-made onslaught
And nature's revenge.

Humans rush
Through the woods, oceans, and plains
Rapidly multiplying
Growing, innovating
Evolving, changing
Taking, and living
Until the host dies,
Then the disease too
Will end.
- How do we all win?

Why do we use scales to represent justice
When balance is treated like a suggestion?

Justice is scales and a rusty chain
Coated in jargon and make-believe
Where the wielder tips the plates
With strategy or whim
In an unknown game
Played amongst their club of marble giants.

The people are not weighed on the scale
But underneath it,
We're scurrying mice
Looking for scraps of food
And hoping all the while
A tipping plate won't fall down and crush us.
-      It shouldn't hurt people

Little lights fill rooms at night,
Clocks, phones, glows under door cracks,
My room never sleeps
So how can I?
   -    The nights before a nap day

What keeps me up?
My mind in a place
Where there are no expectations of me,
A moment I don't have to walk into dread
Like a deer across a road
Or a squirrel with nowhere else to live than sparse trees in
neighborhoods.

I'm a night person
Because I love the night
Because I hate the day,
It's just a case of the Mondays
And Tuesdays
And Wednesdays, Thursdays, Fridays, Saturdays, Sundays
Over and over and over again,
So I stay up
And stop the days from changing.

162

Some nights I can only repeat
I don't want to be here
I don't want to be here
I don't want to be here
I don't want to be here
I don't want to be here
I don't want to be here
    I don't want to be here
I don't want to be here

I don't want to be here

I don't want to be here
  I don't want to be here
  I don't want to be here
I don't want to be here
I don't want to be here

                    The voice in my head hates me
                    The voice in my head wants to
                                Hurt me
                         And I want to let it.

                              Let

                              Me

                              Out.

I don't want to be here
I don't want to be here
I don't want to be here
I don't want to be here
I don't want to be here
  I don't want to be here
  I don't want to be here
I don't want to be here
I don't want to be here
I don't want to be here
I don't want to be here
  I don't want to be here
   I don't want to be here
  I don't want to be here
   I don't want to be here
   I don't want to be here
I don't want to be here
How can I face the morning like that?
          -    The Worst Days of my Life

Optimism is one side of the coin.
The side I can never seem to land on
The side that should feel safe
But doesn't.

Pessimism is the other beast
It's being prepared, being scared,
It isn't expecting the worst to happen,
Though I'm still sure it will.

If your mind and body are floating away from each other
Squeeze your hands between your thighs,
Take yourself out to eat,
Do something that scares you,
Call the friend you haven't seen in a year,
Reorganize your room
Your closet,
And hug yourself until it hurts.
- But don't forget to let go and take a breath

(repeat as necessary)

How many years
Will it take
Before I realize
I'm unhappy?
How many more
Before I make a change?

Leftover illustrations from adapted or lost poems

Early Cover Sketch

168

Author's Note (3/24/2023)

Hi everyone, thank you so much for picking up this book and reaching the end (or skipping to the end, you never know). For a long time, I wasn't sure if this was ever going to exist, though I so desperately needed it to. While I'm writing this, I'm still not sure it's going to happen, but if you're reading it, that's probably a good sign!

There are so many things that writing this collection did for me and my hopefully growing confidence. And there are also many things that reading these approx. 10,000 words over and over and over again made me want to do--like pull all my hair out and stay up all night pretending I was getting something done.

For you though, I hope this collection made you feel something—anything really. I hope it reminded you to reconnect with your feelings and that sometimes you need a moment to complain and cry. I hope for some of you it could offer some moments of catharsis and solidarity.

To be perfectly honest, this project wasn't meant to be a poetry collection at all. Really. There wasn't going to be a single poem. Not one. As the budding novelist I hoped to be, and after many failed attempts, I was going to write a collection of short stories. I didn't pay any attention to the fact that I didn't read short stories. It just felt like a good first step.

When I started at the ripe old age of 20 years old, I thought it would be fun and quirky to make all of the characters of each short story 20 (or 20,000 in one case) and that each might represent a struggle I was facing or an emotion I was having (or a dramatic daydream). Turns out, I couldn't isolate my problems that easily and everything started to blur together.

So, naturally I

- Ditched the short stories
- Started writing down my feelings
    - Which I was having a lot of these days
- Put the narratives on pause for what was quickly being a passion project

For a while, I wrote under an even more dramatic concept *20 Years Drowning*, but it wasn't really the past twenty years of my life that I was writing about, but my continuous present. Before long, I shifted my concept and focus to what you see before you: *Here's To Another Year*.

Thank you again for picking up my very first collection, and I wish you luck in making it through another year.

Cheers!

Acknowledgements

(Winter 2023 Post-New Years)

How do I thank every person in my life (good and bad) for leading me up to this very moment? How do I explain to all of you reading this that even after I've written these very words and it's published and out of my hands that anyone who reads this is absolutely incredible, and that you, in more than a small way, are giving this book life. And for that, I thank you.

If I were to try and cover the history of this collection and everyone who helped me get here, I think I would have to start with (Dr.) Lucia, my literature credit professor, who gave us the option to write a short collection of poetry instead of an essay. An obvious choice on my part, but what I didn't expect was that I would never stop writing poems after that.

I'd like to thank the editors I worked with, Vanessa and Justin for being kind and encouraging on my first work and for pushing me further outside of my comfort zone than I would've walked myself.

Ok, here's the fun, mushy ones that I definitely didn't cry about when I first tried to write this.

My family: My parents, who love and support even when I don't think I want them to; my brother, who always tries to push me forward even through my resistance; our gorgeous troublesome German Shepard Comet (i.e. Cosmo, Stinky, Butt-Butt, Comfetti, Cosmosis, Comet Allez-vous, etc.) who helps me remember that life isn't so serious; my grandma, Mai, who always made me feel at home wherever we were; my cousins, Lan-Anh and Minh-Chau (and Steph who read my collection at one of its earliest stages) who always help me to laugh no matter what mood I'm in; and so many more family members who light up my life. I love all of you so much.

My friends: Sari, Abby, Nic, Alek, Fardowsa, Amanda (special shoutout to her because we met in the class that got me into poetry writing), Shea, Max, Caroline, Elaine, Morgan, and many more who support me through every endeavor, I'm shocked you all have listened to me ramble and stress over writing and art for so many years.

Miscellaneous Adult Figures: Sarah, who shares my anxiety and told me that sometimes you just have to pick your violin back up and play it; Dena, Kristina, and Tamara, who have gone out of their ways to boost me up; Siv, who has been such a gem for so many people in my life, I don't know how to thank you for supporting me unconditionally and being one of my mom and dad's best friends.

And finally, to everyone who willingly spends time with me, thanks for hanging out with me even though I'm such a hater.

Here's to another year, everyone.

About the Author

Hey lovelies, I'm Jesse, but you can call me JJ. I'm a self-published author, artist, and perhaps a budding book witch (which is to say I light candles and mix drinks when I read).

These days when I'm not writing or crying, I'm learning Vietnamese recipes from my family, attempting K-pop dances, or playing Dungeons & Dragons.

This is Simmons' debut collection, written in his latter years of college. Currently based in Ohio.

www.jessebsimmonswrites.com
Instagram: @jesse.b.simmons